Nathan's Story

By

Michael J. McHugh

Great Light Publications

Nathan's Story
Copyright 2010 Great Light Publications

All rights reserved. No part of this book may be reproduced or transmitted in any form or by any means, electronic or mechanical, without the written permission of the publisher. Brief quotations embodied in articles or reviews are permitted.

Written by Michael J. McHugh

Cover and text illustrations by Keith R. Neely

Cover design and layout by Bob Fine

A publication of

Great Light Publications

422 S. Williams Ave.

Palatine, Illinois 60074

www.greatlightpublications.com

ISBN 978-0-9822848-5-8

This book was printed and bound in Canada

Table of Contents

Preface 5

Foreword 7

Chapter 1. Rich Man, Poor Man 9

Chapter 2. For the Love of a Lamb 17

Chapter 3. A Hungry Stranger 21

Chapter 4. The Missing Lamb 25

Chapter 5. The Rich Man's Feast......................................31

Chapter 6. The Righteous Judge 37

Teaching Suggestions 43

Preface

One of the most powerful and memorable scenes recorded in the Bible is the confrontation between King David and the prophet Nathan. At a low point in David's life, when he was straying from God as a prodigal son, the Lord sent just the right person with just the right message to call him back from the path of death to the path of repentance unto life.

The beauty and power of the story that Nathan shared with David is founded, in many respects, upon its absolute simplicity. Regardless of age, race, or cultural heritage, few people need to struggle to comprehend the vital moral principles that flow out of the inspired message that was delivered by Nathan. David himself, even in his anemic spiritual condition, had no difficulty identifying where the lines of justice needed to be drawn with respect to the characters presented in Nathan's story. One man was clearly guilty of multiple transgressions against his neighbor, while the other was just as clearly an innocent victim of another man's callous and unlawful behavior. Little wonder why David, who was both a king and judge in ancient Israel, was so thoroughly convicted when he was informed by Nathan that he "was the man", i.e. the guilty party!

Although the story that follows mirrors, to a certain degree, the biblical narrative that first came from the lips of the prophet Nathan to David, it is not intended to provide readers with a strict or literal retelling of the story recorded in 2 Samuel 12:1-9. Nor, I might add, is this book seeking to present some sort of paraphrased version of this scriptural account. The true goal of *Nathan's Story*, simply put, is to provide children with an edifying story that contains many of the key principles of the original biblical account from Second Samuel.

May Almighty God be pleased to use this simple story, which is based on timeless moral principles, to challenge youngsters of all ages to love their neighbor as themselves to the glory of King Jesus.

Michael J. McHugh
Palatine, Illinois
2010

Foreword

The story you are about to read will provide young children with a powerful example of how the sin of coveting can undermine ones ability to love his neighbor. For this reason, both before and after you read this story to youngsters, it is recommended that you explain the following Scripture passages to them:

"You shall not covet your neighbor's house; you shall not covet your neighbor's wife, nor his male servant, nor his female servant, nor his ox, nor his donkey, nor anything that is your neighbor's."

Exodus 20:17

"Jesus said to him, "You shall love the Lord your God with all your heart, with all your soul, and with all your mind. This is the first and great commandment. And the second is like it: You shall love your neighbor as yourself. On these two commandments hang all the Law and the Prophets."

Matthew 22:37-40

A helpful group of teaching suggestions is provided at the back of the book to aid those who are reading through this story with young children.

Chapter One
Rich Man, Poor Man

Long ago, near a big city, there lived
a rich man and **a poor man**.

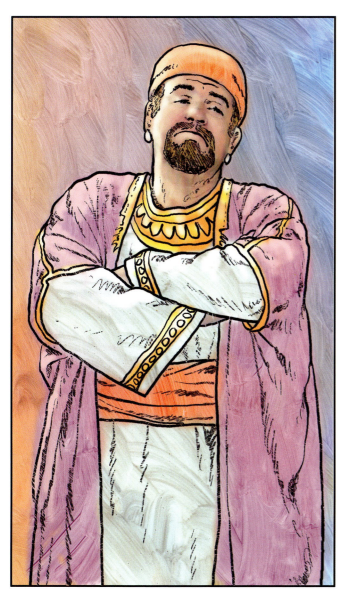

The rich man had nice clothes,
a fancy gold ring,
and a huge home
in the city.

He also owned a large farm just
outside of town that had big barns and many animals.

This man had also been blessed with a loving wife,
five children, and several servants to help him with his work around the farm.

No wonder that people called him a "rich man".

Every day, the rich man loved to walk around his farm and look at his big house, and admire all of the animals in the field.

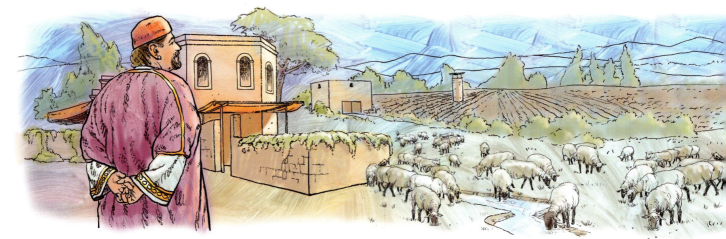

He also liked to take long walks with his wife so they could watch their children play. This man was very proud of all the beautiful things that he owned.

Sometimes, the rich man would ask himself;
"I wonder what I have done to deserve all of these riches?"

The only answer that seemed right to this man, was that his riches must have come to him because he was so wise and good.

The rich man had a neighbor living close to his farm who was very poor.

The poor man lived in a tiny stone house with his two sons.
His wife had died shortly after giving birth to their second son, so the
poor man was very sad and lonely without her.

This father had such a small garden that he could barely feed his children. Day after day, he worked hard just to put food on the table.

One day, the poor man decided to do something to try to bring some joy into his hard life. He decided to go to a small farm near his home, in order to buy a tiny lamb for a pet.

Oh, how happy the father was to carry his new friend home on his shoulders.

Now he would not be so lonely or sad anymore!

Chapter Two

For the Love of a Lamb

It did not take long for the little lamb to feel right at home with his new master. The lamb would follow the poor man around all day long, and keep him company. They would play together in the house, or work together in the yard.

The boys soon taught the tiny creature how to pick up sticks in the yard as well as other tricks. As the days passed, the father and his sons grew to love the small white lamb more and more.

The lamb soon began to eat right at the table, just like a member of the family. The furry creature ate food from the poor man's hand, and drank from his cup.

Most every evening, the lamb would lie in the man's lap and fall asleep while he was being petted.

Even though this father was very poor and owned few things, he would often pray: "Lord, I know that I do not deserve any good thing. Thank you for giving me food to eat, the blessings of sons, and the joy that comes from being with my pet lamb."

Chapter Three

A Hungry Stranger

One day, a traveler came to visit the rich man.

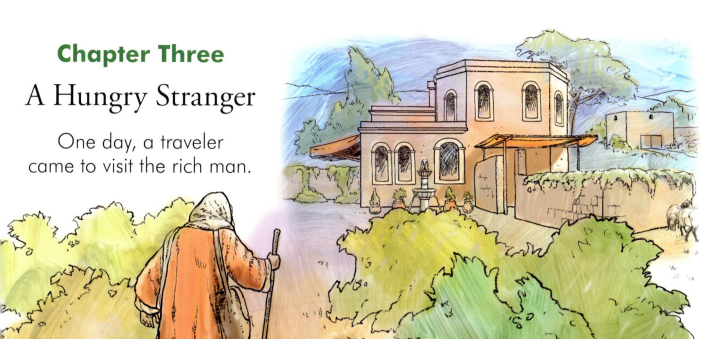

The visitor was hungry, but since he had not told anyone that he was coming, no food had been prepared for him.

As the rich man sat talking with his visitor, he became very sad. The man knew that he needed to be kind to this stranger, but he did not want to kill any of his own animals to feed him. The rich man wanted to have someone else provide the food for his guest.

"I have a great idea," thought the rich man. "My neighbor has a lamb that is fat and in good condition. I do not think that he will miss this one little lamb. I will send my servant over to take him for my feast."

A short time later, the rich man spoke to his servant and said, "Go over to our neighbors and get the fat lamb that is in their yard. I am tired of this animal straying onto our property, in order to eat from our fields. As soon as you come back, prepare the creature for our supper this evening in honor of our guest."

Chapter Four

The Missing Lamb

Early that same evening, the old man returned home to find that his dear lamb was missing. "I wonder where my little lamb has gone. I am so sad that my tiny friend is not here to greet me," he said.

The poor man looked everywhere for his lost lamb.

He searched in his house. He searched in his small yard and garden. Finally, he asked his sons if they knew what had happened to their missing pet.

"Father," said one of the boys, "we have looked all around and we cannot find our tiny friend. I think someone must have come and taken him away. See, it looks like a little blood and fur is over near the corner of our yard.

"I think that our rich neighbor, who is so cruel and mean, is the one who took our pet lamb," added the other son.

"My sons," replied the father, "let us not be so quick to judge our neighbor in this matter. The fact is, we do not have any idea who stole our dear pet lamb."

"Well," asked one of his sons, "what are we going to do now to get back what was stolen?"

"Boys," said the father in reply, "the first thing that we are going to do is to pray.

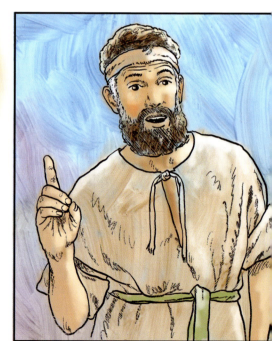

God alone can help us to figure out what to do."

As the poor man and his sons sat down to pray, the father began: "Lord, our hearts are breaking. We are confused and angry, and do not know what to do to find our lamb. I do not understand how anyone could be so cruel as to steal a poor family's only lamb. We ask, Lord, that you would arise and bring to justice those who did this great evil. While we wait on you dear Father, we ask that you would give our hearts peace."

Chapter Five
The Rich Man's Feast

That very evening as planned, the rich man held a feast for his guest. He served him the lamb that had been stolen by his servant a few hours before.

"I trust you are enjoying the meal," said the wicked host, "I only serve the very best meat to my guests."

"I simply cannot tell you when I have had better meat," replied the visitor as he finished his dinner. "You are a very kind and gracious host to feed me so well on such short notice," he added.

Before the rich man could reply to these remarks, however, he and his guest suddenly heard the sound of people crying loudly in the distance.

"Why do your neighbors cry and mourn so loudly?" asked the visitor. "Please tell them to stop, for it upsets me to listen to such things, especially after I have eaten."

33

"How should I know why my foolish neighbors mourn and cry so loudly this night?" replied the rich man.

"I have no dealings with these people, for they are nothing more than poor beggars and thieves," added the host in an angry tone of voice.

"I do not know how you have the patience to put up with neighbors that like to make trouble," replied the guest, trying to calm the rich man down.

"Oh, God alone knows how much I have to go through just to try to be a good neighbor," said the rich host with lying lips. "Let us shut the doors and windows, and move to a quiet part of the house before these people completely ruin our feast."

Chapter Six
The Righteous Judge

A few days after the feast, someone who saw the servant steal the poor man's lamb, reported the crime to the king.

In answer to the prayers of the poor man, the king demanded that the rich man come before him to answer for his wicked deed.

The just and wise king asked the rich man, "How could you order your servant to steal the one and only lamb of a poor neighbor, when you already have so many of your own? Have you no pity in your sinful heart for those who are old and poor?"

"Oh King," replied the rich man, "I am indeed guilty in this matter. I have failed to do what is right."

"As the Lord lives," said the King from his judgement throne, "you deserve to die for your crime. I will, however, grant you the mercy that you failed to give to your neighbor by sparing your life. Your duty now is to restore to your neighbor what you have stolen. I order you, therefore, to give your poor neighbor four of your best lambs to pay for what you have unlawfully taken."

"May God help me to turn away from my foolish ways, and to love mercy more than worldly gain," said the rich man.

After the rich man gave the four sheep to his poor neighbor, he also invited him and his sons to a great feast. This time, however, the guests of honor were none other than the old man and his children!

And in the days that followed, the Lord did give this rich man the grace and spiritual strength to turn from his wicked ways. He also granted him the ability to begin to love his neighbor even more than he loved himself.

And so, by the grace of Almighty God, they all lived happily ever after.

The End

TEACHING SUGGESTIONS

The following information can be useful to teachers who wish to help young children to comprehend the main truths or biblical principles contained in *Nathan's Story*. It is recommended that instructors utilize these suggestions after they have first read the story to the children, as well as the Bible passages listed in the Foreword.

Chapter One
Rich Man, Poor Man

Scripture Reading: 1 Timothy 6:17-18; Matthew 25:1-30; James 4:1-6

Young children need to be taught that the world will always be filled with both rich people and poor people. Remind youngsters that the Word of God never condemns someone merely because he is rich or poor. The Scriptures do, however, set forth the principle of "...to whom much is given, from him much will be required." (Luke 12:48) The Lord, therefore, requires that His creatures be good stewards over that which has been entrusted to them — whether they have much or little. Read the Parable of the Ten Virgins and the Parable of the Talents from Matthew 25 with your student(s), and discuss the importance of God's people using the time and talents that the Lord provides wisely.

The Bible encourages people not to think more highly of themselves than they should, but to be clothed with the virtue of humility. The Word of God also warns men not to be prideful by declaring in Proverbs 16:18, "Pride goes before destruction, and a haughty spirit before a fall." In the case of the rich man in our story, the real underlying sin that blinded him from being able to recognize his duty to love his neighbor was his pride. Talk with your student(s) about the sin of pride and its destructive fruits. Help them to recognize how pride breeds selfishness, as well as contention and strife with their fellow man. It is a true and faithful saying that, "God resists the proud, but gives grace to the humble." (James 4:6)

At the close of chapter one, the reader is introduced to a poor man who is a widower. He is described as being sad and lonely of heart after losing his beloved wife. Ask your student(s) if they know what it means to be lonely. Help them to recognize that one of the first things that God identified as "not good" soon after He created human beings was loneliness. Almighty God declared in Genesis after He made Adam, that it "…was not good for man to be alone." Read James 1:27 and Lev. 19:32-34 to your student(s), and encourage them to make it part of their mission in life to help those who are struggling with loneliness, particularly in cases where they come across widows and orphans. Even when children are playing with other youngsters from their community, they should be encouraged to go out of their way to try to include everyone that wants to join them in their activities or games.

Chapter Two
For the Love of a Lamb

Scripture Reading: Genesis 1: 24-31; Deut. 25:4; Proverbs 12:10

The Bible teaches us that the Lord placed animals on the earth primarily for the service of man, so that these creatures would be a blessing to mankind. Sadly, after the fall of man, not all creatures remained a blessing to the human race. Nevertheless, most animals are still quite useful or profitable to men even if it is only for companionship.

The opening of chapter two presents the touching story of the relationship that existed between a lonely man and his tiny lamb. The little creature was chosen as his pet, for the poor man needed companionship at this stage of his life even more than he needed more meat on his table.

Although few children struggle with the sin of being cruel or neglectful to animals, nevertheless, it is still helpful to remind youngsters of the fact that the Bible forbids cruelty to animals. Read Proverbs 12:10 and Duet. 25:4 to your student(s) and discuss why it is wrong to torture or starve any creature.

Chapter Three
A Hungry Stranger

Scripture Reading: Luke 10: 25-37; Micah 6:8; 1 Peter 2:15-25; Romans 12: 9-21

It is a sad testimony to fallen human nature that so often we are more kind and considerate to strangers than we are to those who live right next door to us. The vital truth that young people need to recognize, however, is that God commands us to love everyone who comes in our path as our neighbor. We must love people, regardless of the community or background that they happen to come from.

Read the story of the Good Samaritan from Luke 10 to your student(s) in order to help them understand how to identify who is their neighbor. No less than eight times, the Word of God commands people to "love their neighbor." This principle of life is one of the most frequently repeated passages in all of Holy Scripture, therefore, impress upon children the need to recognize how important this commandment is to Almighty God.

Help students to see that loving their neighbor begins when they esteem the needs of others more highly than their own desires. In other words, loving one's neighbor demands that people abandon a selfish or self-centered attitude toward life and living. Children need to recognize that because God loves sinful men, He has called and empowered His servants to "go and do thou likewise." Encourage your student(s) to understand and be thankful for the fact that the Lord does not give people the choice to love others. All men are commanded to love their neighbor in a manner that is consistent with God's truth. (Matthew 4:4)

Discuss the fact that all men are called to love their neighbor, whether such ones are easy to love or difficult. God certainly understands that some people will not appreciate the efforts of those who are trying to love them and will not respond in a loving manner, nevertheless, God still directs His servants to extend love to them. The Lord has called His people to overcome evil with good in their relationships with others, as well as in every area of life. God desires that His children put to silence the foolishness of sinful men by doing acts of love and service toward all that they meet.

The final principle in chapter three that children should be taught concerns the sin of coveting. Help your student(s) to comprehend that the sin of coveting that the rich man engaged in is a violation of the Tenth Commandment which states: "You shall not covet your neighbor's house; you shall not covet your neighbor's wife, nor his male servant, nor his female servant, nor his ox, nor his donkey, nor anything that is your neighbor's."(Exodus 20:17)

We covet when we desire to have something that is not lawfully ours. Coveting takes place when we are not content with what God has provided for us at a given point and we, therefore, begin to lust after something that our neighbor possesses. Close this lesson by reading Romans 13:9 to your student(s).

Chapter Four
The Missing Lamb

Scripture Reading: 2 Timothy 3:1-12; Proverbs 14:15; 2 Cor. 4:5-10

The major principles that your student(s) needs to grasp in chapter four center upon three points:

1. How to handle adversity in a biblical manner

2. The importance of not rushing into judgement against another

3. The value of prayer as a means of casting our cares upon the Lord in order that He might be glorified (Read Psalm 91 and Luke 11:1-13)

Jesus clearly taught that in this world we shall have tribulation, i.e. trouble (John 16:33). Help your student(s) to comprehend that one of the primary reasons why God has not chosen to remove His people from the earth immediately after their conversion, is that He desires to mature His people **through** problems, rather than saving them **from** all of life's problems. For this reason, it is vital for youngsters to learn how to biblically work through adversity in a Christ-honoring manner. God has indeed ordained that His children pick up a cross in order to follow Him, so that they may inherit a crown of glory in heaven.

Chapter Five
The Rich Man's Feast

Scripture Reading: James 4:14-17; Matthew 7:12; Proverbs 28:13; Galatians 6:7-10

The Bible states, "Therefore, to him who knows to do good and does not do it, to him it is sin." (James 4:17) The rich man depicted in chapter five knew very well God's commands concerning hospitality, yet he clearly chose to steal from one man in order to lead his guest to think that he was kind and gracious. Help your student(s) to see that true love and hospitality does not work evil against another person. Read Romans 13:10, and discuss how the Bible supports the principle that "the end does not justify the means." Emphasize that God's people are not at liberty to do evil so that good may come from it. The golden rule found in Matthew 7:12, for example, must never be violated in order to fulfill one's duty to show hospitality to a stranger.

Another important principle found in the latter portion of chapter five, is that whenever anyone tries to hide his sin he will not prosper. Worldly gain or success that is achieved through wickedness has a foundation made out of sand. Sooner or later, Almighty God will destroy the house of sin that sinners seek to build. Assist your student(s) to see that if they desire to have true lasting success, they must build their lives and relationships upon the solid and upright foundation of God's Holy Word. This is true, because God Himself plainly declares, "Be sure that your sins will find you out," and also, "Do not be deceived, God is not mocked; for whatever a man sows, that he will also reap." (Galatians 6:7)

Chapter Six
The Righteous Judge

Scripture Reading: 1 John 1:9; 2 Samuel 12:1-13; Matthew 18:11-14; Philippians 2:1-11

When the rich man in our story was brought before the righteous judge to answer for his crime, he confessed his sin and did not try to justify his wicked actions. He was willing to take responsibility for his foolish deeds, and to do what the judge required in order to make things right with his neighbor. The proud rich man must have found it difficult and embarrassing to swallow his pride in order to confess his sin. This act, however, was the very thing that God used to turn his life around for good. (1 John 1:9)

The Bible clearly teaches that if a sinner is willing to confess and forsake his sin, the Lord will respond with cleansing and forgiveness. Help your student(s) to understand that God will never cast off a sinner who is truly seeking to repent from his sins. The path of mercy and grace is open to those who have the wisdom to seek forgiveness from the Lord, as well as from those that they offend. In fact, God requires that we extend forgiveness to those who are willing to repent from their sins and be reconciled with us. Instructors should read and discuss Matthew 18: 21-35 with their student(s).

The final suggestion at the close of this chapter, is for teachers to read and talk about the actual Bible story that depicts the confrontation between King David and the prophet Nathan that is recorded in 2 Samuel 12: 1-13.